THE LONG NIGHT OF THE SUCCUBUS

By Darian Cyan

ADULTS ONLY

This is a work of fiction. Names, characters, places, and incidents either are the product of the author's imagination or are used fictitiously. Any resemblance to actual persons, living or dead, events, or locales is entirely coincidental.

ISBN: 9781709491351

Copyright © 2021 by Darian Cyan

All rights reserved. No part of this book may be reproduced or used in any manner without written permission of the copyright owner except for the use of quotations in a book review.

Book design by Darian Cyan
*Art by Venomarts00_*

THE LONG NIGHT OF THE SUCCUBUS

The woman Brant most desired was getting away while he was stuck in a tedious, nonsensical conversation. The office Christmas party bubbled around him, a congregation of co-workers Brant knew, knew to say hello to, or did not know at all, stood around in cliques chatting about he did not care what. Alcohol hung heavy in the air and on the breath of Patrick Longman, who was drunker than most. Patrick kept grabbing Brant's shoulder to keep him from leaving. Brant had said, "I'll see you on Monday" five times already. Patrick ignored him and grabbed his shoulder again. The man's voice slurred so much from intoxication Brant could not understand a word.

Stephanie moved across the room to the exit, saying goodbye to people as she went. Tonight was his chance. Tonight was the night Brant intended to ask her out. If he could meet her in the elevator or on the street outside, just the two of them, it would be perfect.

Brant turned away from Patrick. Patrick grabbed his shoulder. The sudden urge to punch the drunk in the face nearly overwhelmed him.

Stephanie, half Chinese, half Filipina, was the most delightful woman Brant had ever met. She moved across the room; the shining black silk of her long hair played across her shoulders whenever she turned to say something sweet. Everything Stephanie said was sweet.

Best of all, Brant knew she was single.

He watched her get to the door and turned to follow. Patrick grabbed his shoulder again. Brant turned back to say, "Oh for fuck's sake!" when he got bumped hard from behind and stumbled forward. The hit had been on his backside. The soft globes of somebody else's posterior rammed into his.

When he regained his balance, he turned to see Kaho Nakagawa, an upper manager Brant only knew by sight. A Japanese woman in her late forties, she wore large round glasses, her dark brown hair tied neatly back in a ponytail and a tight skirt suit. Her reputation for strictness and a cutting tongue frightened everyone.

Brant opened his mouth to apologise when she got there first.

"Oh, Brant," she said. "I'm so sorry."

It surprised him that Ms Nakagawa even knew his name.

"Oh, no. It's quite all right."

Her daughter, Miho, stood beside her. Miho was nineteen or thereabouts. She did not work with her mother but had come to the office party. A shorter and slimmer woman, her hair was black and cut to her jawline. She watched Brant now with an amused expression.

Without meaning to, he appreciated her figure. She wore tight black jeans and an even tighter T-shirt advertising some heavy metal band with a bat motif. Her hands held a drink in front of her breasts. The small protuberances of her nipples shaped the T-shirt fabric.

"I think you were leaving?" Ms Nakagawa said.

He snapped out of his ogling. He should slap his own face for checking out a boss's daughter right in front of her. Ms Nakagawa and Miho watched him with the same smile. A smile of a shared joke or insight. She knew his name, and Brant felt she and her daughter knew a lot more.

Ms Nakagawa stepped forward and whispered into his ear, "If you hurry now, you might still catch her."

Brant tried to keep his face neutral. Miho's smile widened.

He nodded and turned for the door.

Patrick, still mumbling, made a grab for his shoulder again. Ms Nakagawa took Patrick's arm and held it. "Patrick, you've talked to Brant enough." Her voice was like ice.

Patrick mumbled some more but stepped back. Brant took his chance.

In the lobby, the elevator door closed. He sprinted to it and jabbed the button five times. The door opened.

Stephanie smiled at him. "Oh, hi. Going home?"

They were alone. Perfect.

"Yes. I've had enough." He stood beside her. The cloud of her perfume sent a thrill through him.

"Yeah," Stephanie said. "I'm not a drinker and there is only so much small talk I can take." She stared down at something she held in her hands. A lottery ticket.

"You like the lottery?"

"Hm." She twisted the ticket and rubbed her thums over it. "When I was at university some of the other students used to run a secret lottery. We would pass tickets around to each other under the tables during lectures. I guess that's when I started."

Now. Now was the time to ask her.

"So, what do you like to do when you're not in the office and not playing the lottery?" Smooth, Brant. If they gave out awards for seduction, he would win the booby prize. A No-Booby prize, like a Fleshlight.

"I do non-office things." She looked at him side-on and gave him a smile like the ones Kaho Nakagawa and her daughter had a few minutes earlier.

"You're going to make me guess, aren't you?"

"You're the one who wants to know," she said, teasing him.

Five floors left to go. "Okay, you like to go to church and sing in the choir." Oh, dear God...

Stephanie raised an eyebrow. "You're half-right."

"You like karaoke?"

She nodded. "Yeah, sometimes. Not bad."

Now, Brant! Do it now! "Would you like to go to karaoke with me sometime?"

"Can you sing?" The elevator door opened, and Stephanie stepped out.

Brant followed her. "Umm...no."

"Then why would I go to karaoke with you?"

"I can listen to you sing." He had the vexatious feeling of something slipping out of his grasp.

"No, thanks, I like to sing by myself." They went through the lobby doors and out onto the street.

"Then how about dinner together? A movie?"

Stephanie stopped and faced him. Her smile did not have its usual bright energy. "I'm sorry, Brant. I don't think it's a good idea. Thanks for asking me though."

The tight pants of her business suit moved away, taking his

hopes with them.

He took a long way home to walk off the disappointment and frustration. Weeks. Weeks to work up the courage and more to get the opportunity, only to run into a wall at the end. Even with no confidence with women, Brant had been sure she would say yes. Now he realised his attraction to her was obsessive, and he had fooled himself it was mutual. Stephanie smiled brightly at *everyone*, was nice to *everyone*, he was foolish to think she reserved her brightest smile for him.

He sighed and walked on. Without knowing why, he took a side street he usually ignored. The architecture along the road was older, and he wondered why he never noticed it before. It had been an avenue of small businesses once. Old shops with roofs covering the footpaths ran along in front of their dirty shop windows. Most were closed and likely abandoned, but yellow light came from the windows of one. The board above the shop read, *Grandmother's Old Things. Antiques and Oddities of the Past.*

Brant stopped. A sign hung on the brass door handle read 'Open'. He reached for the handle, expecting it to be locked, but it turned. A bell rang as he pushed the door.

Inside, the air smelled of dust and old papers, along with a few vague scents of lacquer and old wood. Tall shelves stacked close together were piled with knickknacks and books. Brant advanced between them carefully to avoid knocking any item down with his shoulders. At the shop counter, an old woman sat behind an antique cash register reading a hardcover book without a dust jacket. She looked up at him over her reading glasses.

"Can I help you?" she asked.

"Ah, I just came in to browse. I was surprised to find your shop open at this time of night."

"I only open at night. Was there any particular type of item you were interested in?"

"No, I was more curious than anything. I did not know this place existed."

"Everyone who comes in here is looking for a particular item.

Even if they do not know it. Why don't you browse as you intended? Whatever you're searching for will find you. It usually does."

The old lady's sales pitch intrigued him. Brant felt obligated to find something to purchase before he left. Anything cheap and appealing would do. He turned left and went to the farthest wall of the shop. Old clocks were shoved on the same shelves as old books, along with magazines, statuettes, carvings, music boxes, pocketknives and small caskets. As he browsed the dusty shelves and their compelling mess, he noticed a calm coming over him. The longer he stayed there, the more he caught himself zoning out. Twice he shook his head to snap himself awake.

He examined a pile of several daggers stained with rust. Behind these sat a longsword. Eager to find something to purchase so he could leave, Brant reached for it.

"That is not what you want," the shopkeeper called from behind the counter.

Brant pulled his hand back. He searched above him for security cameras or mirrors. The only technology on the ceiling were incandescent bulbs throwing down weak amber light.

"Why don't you look at the figurine in the next aisle?"

Brant followed her suggestion. He found one figurine in the aisle. An obsidian statuette of a naked woman with twisted horns and large bat wings coming from her back. She stood with her legs apart on a round base. In her right hand, she held a multi-tailed whip, in her left a wand.

Brant looked closer. No, not a wand, a phallus. The expression on the woman's face was an aspect of utter mischievousness.

"That is the item you want," the old lady said.

Brant jumped. She stood right beside him.

"I'm not sure."

"She is the succubus," the old lady whispered. "A granter of carnal wishes. She is the one you seek."

Brant stared at the shopkeeper.

"She will bring you what you desire if you summon her. Even the wishes you would not admit to yourself." The old woman's softly spoken words added to the shop's soporific atmosphere.

"How do I summon her?" he whispered, becoming a party to the weird conspiracy of the succubus figure.

The old lady leaned close to his ear. "As a man, you must anoint her with your seed. Pleasure yourself onto her. Splash her with your excretions. She will come."

Brant's drowsiness was not so strong he failed to be shocked. An old lady had just told him to masturbate and ejaculate onto an antique statue to summon some wish-granting sex creature.

"Umm..."

"Fifty dollars."

Brant's hands held the succubus statuette. He had no memory of having picked it up. He nodded.

Lying on his couch, he stared at the statuette sitting on his coffee table. He could not just jerk off, come all over a statue and expect his wishes to be granted.

The obsidian figure watched him, her expression absolutely confident as if they were playing poker and she held a royal flush, and he only held a pair of twos. The whip in her right hand, a tool of a sexuality he had never considered, disturbed him.

Liar.

The thought came in his own voice, but it was as if another had spoken. There were fantasies . . . Lying over the knees of a woman . . . always an older woman, mature but beautiful and strong . . . of holding a whip himself . . .

The image of Stephanie came to him. Naked and lying over the back of his couch, presenting her smooth round behind . . .

The grin on the succubus seemed to have widened. Brant unzipped his pants and closed his eyes. The fantasy jumped about. He held the whip and swung it at Stephanie's ass, striping it with red . . . He lay over another woman's knees and received his own punishment . . . he fucked two, then three different women . . .

His hand moved faster. The scattered fantasy carried more power than his usual mental porn and the climax came suddenly. He opened his eyes, saw the statue and thought: *Ah, what the hell.*

He kneeled on the floor and grabbed the obsidian figure as he ejaculated.

Most of it drenched the fifty-dollar antique, the rest hit the floor. After his orgasm subsided, he cursed. He hated cleaning up semen.

He wiped the floor but left the statue stowed with its mess in the bottom of his closet.

Brant awoke sometime in the night. He tried to imagine Stephanie's warm body lying beside him. Giving up, he rolled onto his back. Orange streetlight shone in through his window. He knew every shadow there should be in the room, his body locked rigid when he saw one that should not be there.

A figure stood in his bedroom doorway.

The shadow moved. It did not move with steps but glided toward him. At the end of his bed, it rose into the air and over his sheets to come into the light shining through the window.

Brant's heart thudded. The succubus statue or the woman the statue represented levitated above him. Huge bat wings stretched out behind her. She held the phallus and the whip. The whip's tails she played across the sheets at the level of Brant's groin.

"Are you sure?" Her voice oscillated in the air and tickled Brant's penis.

"About what?" He could not move. A dream, it had to be. A terribly vivid and lucid dream.

He hoped it was a dream.

"You summoned me. I need to hear it from your mouth that you are sure this is what you want."

Every word she spoke stimulated his erogenous zones. His penis, nipples and even his anus vibrated pleasantly. Her body, so lithe and smooth, entranced him. Her breasts, the thick, shining black hair on her mons were impossibly perfect. In the air, a potently stimulating perfume mingled with the scent of female arousal.

Yes, this is what he wanted. "Yes, I'm sure."

"Very well. I will send them to you." Her wings flapped, she turned and vanished.

Brant's eyes snapped open. He jumped out of bed, switched on the light and searched the room, then his apartment. No succubus and nobody else invaded his home.

It had been a dream. He opened the closet and found the figure where he left it. Touching the smooth stone, he found the stickiness was gone.

The statue was clean of his semen.

Monday came and after a weekend of long rambling walks, Netflix and pornography, Brant returned to work. His interactions with Stephanie became awkward. He did his best to behave as if their conversation of Friday night had never taken place, but she looked at him differently now. A new glint in her eyes made him feel like a beta-male loser. At the end of the day, he held back when everyone else left, pretending to clean his desk so he would not have to get into the elevator with her. From the corner of his eye, he watched her leave the office. Ten minutes later he followed.

Brant got in the elevator alone, but as the doors closed Ms Nakagawa jumped in.

"Just made it," she said. "Good afternoon, Brant. How are you today?"

"I'm fine, thank you." He did not want to be alone with the upper manager, especially after the incident at the party. What Kaho Nakagawa said next increased his discomfiture a great deal further.

"We both know that's not true."

"I'm sorry?"

"Don't pretend," she said with her icicle, no-nonsense tone. "Stephanie turned you down. You've been twisting inside trying not to look at her all day while sneaking glances at her sweet, round ass."

Brant could not respond. Ms Nakagawa's perception and observation verged on being a superpower.

"Don't be afraid." She smiled. "I quite understand what you are going through. Men like you are a speciality of mine."

"What do you mean?" Brant hated how timid he sounded.

"You're going to find out exactly what I mean. Beginning now. You are coming to dinner with me."

"I'm not sure I . . ."

"It was not a request, Brant." Her voice cut into him like a whip.

"Yes, Miss. I mean, Ms Nakagawa!"

She laughed and took his hand. "Relax. We are both going to enjoy this. It's what you wanted after all."

Ms Nakagawa took him to a Chinese restaurant with private rooms. As they waited for their orders, she asked him, "What do you like?"

"Regarding what?"

"I know you like Stephanie's firm ass." She watched him closely. "But do you like young women exclusively? Do you like the softer globes of an older woman? Do you only prefer the rounder buttocks of someone like Stephanie, or does the posterior of a girl with slim hips also catch your eye? Do you only like the gentle curves of the buttocks, the smooth cushion they make or do you also have an interest in the puckered plaything in between them?"

Brant wondered if a conversation like this with a female manager constituted sexual harassment. He tried to keep his face neutral.

Under Ms Nakagawa's highly perceptive eye, it made no difference.

She grinned. "Ahh. I see you do. And what do you like to have done to you?"

Brant tried to swallow. The waitress brought them plates of food, and while she served them, Ms Nakagawa smiled at him like a cat smiling at a mouse. Brant felt a gentle rubbing at his groin. Her stockinged foot rested on his chair between his legs. She stroked her toes up and down over his fly.

"Eat up. When you are finished, we are going to find out."

Brant's dinner with Ms Nakagawa went by in a haze. In another move that disoriented him further, she turned the conversation back to the usual mundane topics, and if not for her foot occasionally rubbing at his groin, he would almost have thought he imagined the whole earlier conversation. When he finished eating, he massaged her foot. She purred her appreciation. He finished one; she replaced it with the other and he began again.

Outside the restaurant, Ms Nakagawa took his hand and led him to a taxi.

She sat primly beside him as the ride began, but her left hand reached across and stroked his crotch. His penis soon responded. She traced the hard line of it to the head and circled her fingertip around and around with a feather touch.

"Will you come in your pants if I keep doing this," she whispered to him.

Brant prayed the driver could not hear her.

"Will you squirt your hot fluid into your underwear? It's all right, sweetie. Let go and come if you want to."

The taxi ride ended before any orgasmic crisis could humiliate him.

Ms Nakagawa lived in a small, neat house in a quiet and dark suburban street. The front garden was a forest. They ducked under low-hanging branches and brushed by shrubbery. Silence and the ticking of a clock greeted them when they entered. He hoped Miho was out and would not be home for hours. He did not want to imagine the girl's reaction to ... whatever her mother planned to do to him.

Ms Nakagawa removed her shoes and told to Brant do the same before leading him into her living room. She switched on a single, dim, light. A side cabinet of black wood stood against one wall, and a large couch sitting in the centre of the room were the only furniture. A red Persian rug sat on the floor between the couch and the sideboard. The only other item in the room was an old grandmother clock.

The clock tick-tocked in the silence as Ms Nakagawa disrobed. She removed her jacket, the shirt beneath, then loosened the belt on her skirt and dropped everything to the floor. She wore black pantyhose, black panties, and a matching bra. She undressed in a business-like manner, ignoring him.

Her mature beauty casually unveiled sparked his arousal, but his arousal grew along with his incredulity and fear. He might not have a job the next day if he failed to please her or if he refused her advances.

As she unclipped her bra, she glanced at him. "Get undressed." Her voice returned to its sharp and clipped tone.

Brant had been given an order. He resigned himself to his fate and began to undress, with his eyes still on her body. Her bra came off and her large breasts sunk on her chest.

She stood there watching him in her panties and pantyhose. "Perhaps this will move you along." She turned around and Brant saw the line of a G-string running between her firm buttocks. "Do you like what you see?"

"Yes." He stripped the rest of his clothes off and stood naked before her, embarrassed by his erection and feeling vulnerable.

Ms Nakagawa came closer and examined his penis. "It's beautiful," she whispered. She ran her fingers lightly along the bottom from the base, over the head and back over the top to the thick dark hairs.

"Now," she said. "Time for some instruction."

She went to the sideboard cabinet and opened it. Reaching in, she brought out a long wooden ruler and swung it down into her left palm twice. *Crack! Crack!*

Brant looked at the ruler in her hand and became much more aware of his nudity.

"I am going to ask you what you like. What you *want*. If you hesitate or lie to me, it will mean ten strokes of the ruler."

"You can't be serious!"

"Ahh, the first hesitation. You know perfectly well I *am* serious. And *I* know perfectly well what it is you want. Have you forgotten, dear? Two nights ago, you masturbated and ejaculated onto the fetish of my queen. What did you see, Brant, while you stroked yourself alone?"

Brant's eyes went wide.

Ms Nakagawa smiled. "Now you begin to understand."

"How could you? I... it's just a statue!"

"My queen came to you, did she not?"

"It was a dream!"

Ms Nakagawa laughed.

"But you've been in the office for months! I don't understand how you're involved."

"We come from a place outside of time, Brant, dear. We've always known about your desires, your decision and the summoning of us. I told you: men like you are my speciality."

Brant tried to think, to understand. "But are you saying the succubus sent you to me?"

"Yes."

"But you're... not a succubus. Do you worship the succubus?" Even as he spoke the words, he knew how stupid it sounded.

"Brant, darling, the night has barely begun."

Ejaculating onto a fifty-dollar statue had been silly, an erratic act during a moment of private arousal. Now he questioned what it entered him into. A deal with a succubus, a type of demon.

His penis drooped.

"Oh, don't be afraid, Brant." Ms Nakagawa looked at his weakening member. "I am here to give you what you want. Nothing more, or less. Now, you have already earned ten strokes. Let us continue. Tell me, what do you want to do to me first?"

The clock's ticking marked the time while he tried to make sense of the situation. Ms Nakagawa watched him intently. At some point in the day, or maybe during that walk home on Friday night, he must have stepped out of reality. He examined the upper manager as she stood before him wearing only her black pantyhose and the satin, G-string panties beneath. His penis began to regain its vigour. He wanted her; he could not deny it.

"I want to kiss you," he said, in an attempt to make the situation somehow romantic, or at least closer to normal.

"Twenty strokes. You do want to kiss me, but not *first*. I know your every filthy desire. All you have to do to make them come true is to say them. I will ask you again: What do you want to do to me *first*?"

His mouth went dry. He blurted out the words before she could add another ten strokes. "I want to smell your . . . body."

"What part of my body? Say it clearly, Brant, the way you want to say it."

"I want to . . ." He hesitated. "I want to smell your cunt and asshole through your panties and pantyhose."

"There now. That was easy, wasn't it? Come then. Come and smell me."

Brant needed reassurance she completely understood his request.

"I'm waiting," she said.

Feeling light in the stomach, he dropped to his knees, crawled the few paces to where she stood and pushed his face to her vulva. He breathed in the aromas of her sex and her sweat permeating her underwear and the pantyhose mesh.

She moved her legs wider apart, and he pushed his head between her thighs. He licked at her mons and the bulge of her labia. He turned over and sat on the rug. Reaching up between her thighs, he placed his palms against her hips and pulled her bottom back into his face, driving his nose up into the crevice between her buttocks. He drew in the pungent aroma of her anus and deep crevice sweat. Brant sniffed and sucked it all in. The heat of her buttocks warmed his face, he pushed harder against the round flesh and breathed in more and more. His penis became so hard it might burst.

Taking all he could, he dropped back to the floor and lay there looking up at her ass.

Ms Nakagawa turned around and gazed down at him. "Isn't it so much better when you tell me the truth?"

Brant, breathing heavily, nodded.

"Now," she said. "What else do you want?"

"Your nipples."

She moved away and sat on the couch. "Come and suckle."

Brant crawled to her again. He kneeled on the floor by the couch, took a breast in each hand and moved his mouth to the right nipple. She purred as he teased the dark protuberance with his tongue. The nipple became erect and lengthened. He suckled it like a child at first, but soon his actions became urgent, and he tightened his lips hard around it. Ms Nakagawa made little mewls in a whiny pitch. Her hands reached under him and he felt her fingertips on his penis.

He moved to the other breast and began sucking and licking. From one breast to the other he went, squeezing them in his hands and pushing the nipples up into his mouth. Her breasts became drenched in his saliva.

Ms Nakagawa stroked him faster. Brant tore his face away from her chest.

"I want to watch you undress," he said.

"Hmm." She smiled.

Brant got off her, and she stood up.

"I think you should remove these." She pinched at the fabric of her pantyhose.

On his knees, Brant took the edge of the pantyhose and began rolling them down over her hips and legs. She lifted first one foot from the ground and then another. He rolled the mesh over her heels and off her feet.

Brant stood up. He found the gusset of the pantyhose and buried his nose in it. He sniffed her sex's scent while he watched her remove her last item of clothing.

She turned around and with her back to him, hooked her thumbs into the waistband of her panties, bent forward and lowered the garment down. The narrow black fabric peeled out from her crevice and unveiled her labia and anus.

She turned back to him and tossed the G-String. He caught it and sniffed.

"And now?"

"I want to lick you."

Ms Nakagawa laid back down on her couch and opened her legs.

Brant dropped the underwear and wasted no time getting his face between her thighs.

Natural, thick fur covered her mons.

"Do you like it?" Ms Nakagawa asked. "So many young women these days shave off everything."

"I love it," he murmured into the heat. "I like it natural like this."

"I thought you might." He heard a smile in her voice.

He kissed her labia, tasted them and lapped them before forcing his tongue into the slick valley between. He wriggled it, dragged it upwards and sucked at her wetness. Her moans returned and became little squeals when he found her clitoris.

Brant lifted her knees to her chest, to expose her sex as much as he could, and drove his face in. His tongue licked up and down the length of it, from her perineum to her clitoris and back, going lower each time.

"You want my asshole, don't you?" Ms Nakagawa asked.

Brant's cheeks warmed. He did not answer.

"Ten more strokes, my dear."

"Yes."

"Then lick my little hole, sweetie."

Brant's heart fluttered as he licked down over her perineum and onto the tight ring.

Ms Nakagawa pushed him back and off her just far enough to roll over and present her ass to him, she kneeled low, and her buttocks splayed wide. Brant dove into them and licked her crevice from her pussy to the small of her back and down again.

"This is what you've wanted for so long, isn't it?" She moved away from him and turned back. Getting up on her knees above him, she said, "You poor thing." She took hold of the back of his head with her left hand. Her right hand on his chin forced his mouth open. She drooled spit, a white line of it sank to his lips. Her fingers pushed it into his mouth.

"Now what?" she asked.

"Suck my cock."

"And?"

"I don't..."

"Ten more strokes."

"Lick my asshole." He spoke the request in a timid whisper.

"Of course, dear."

Brant kneeled face down on the couch. Ms Nakagawa kneeled behind him, between his legs and over him. He felt her breasts push into his back as she began kissing the nape of his neck. Her little kisses moved down his spine. The lower they travelled, the more his excitement grew. She cupped his balls and licked his buttocks. Her lips reached the top of his crevice, her tongue slipped between them and slid down over his anus to the back of his balls, leaving a trail of moisture. The caress moved up again and poked at his ring, pushed against it, tickled it. Her other hand took his penis and stroked it while she licked him.

"No one... has ever... done that to me before," he whispered.

Ms Nakagawa stopped her anal kissing long enough to say, "But you always wanted it." He felt the warm breath of her words on his anus, then her tongue tickling him again.

Ms Nakagawa turned over, lay down on the couch and slid her head between his legs. She positioned herself with his cock against her mouth, opened it and took him in.

He looked down and watched her fellate him. Her right hand held his balls, her left moved up to continue to tickle his asshole with her middle finger.

She moved faster, sucking him harder and harder.

Brant felt himself losing control. "No, wait," he said, too late. The excitement of the strange liason, of having his deepest fantasies come true, got to him. He lost control and his penis jerked and pumped.

Ms Nakagawa stroked him, speed making her hand a blur, while he ejaculated over her face.

"I want to..." His vision flickered. It appeared as if two long black twisted horns grew from Ms Nakagawa's head. He blinked, and the image faded.

"I know, sweetie." She let go of his penis and started pushing his semen from her cheeks and lips into her mouth. "You wanted to fuck me. You will. We have all night." She finished cleaning her face and swallowed. "But for the moment, you have punishment coming."

Ms Nakagawa sat on the couch holding the wooden ruler in her right hand. Brant stood before her, feeling weak and ashamed. He slipped his hands across his groin, covering himself.

Ms Nakagawa laughed. "And after all we've done so far. Come, lay across my lap. Just like you've always wanted."

He went to her, kneeled on the couch and lay himself across her. A naughty child stripped naked and humbly accepting his punishment.

Her fingers played across his ass with feather touches. "Forty strokes. Are you ready?"

God, yes. Ready to be laid down over the knees of an older woman, naked. Ready to be spanked. He would never have told another living soul about this fantasy, but Ms Nakagawa already knew everything he wanted. She knew when he held back, she knew what he wanted before he said it.

"Yes, I am ready." He braced his hands against the armrest.

"I think you want to say that differently, don't you?"

He did, but a vestige of pride made him hesitate.

"Fifty strokes, sweetie."

"I am ready, mistress. Please spank me."

"Very good. I think from now on you can call me Mistress Kaho. Now, you will count the strokes."

Mistress Kaho lifted the wooden ruler, brought it down again softly across the middle of his buttocks, lifted it, brought it down softly again.

Then she struck.

The sting came a second after the sound. "One!" He winced.

"Only forty-nine more to go," she told him in a gentle, encouraging voice. Her left hand stroked his hair.

The next strokes came faster, but just as hard. She placed them across his buttocks more-or-less evenly, but whenever a strike hit him in the same place twice or more at once, the stinging grew rapidly. Where he was not struck, he burned, and when he was struck there again the burning turned to intense stinging.

Counting and keeping count became so much more difficult than he imagined. He yelled, grunted and gasped out the words. The longer the spanking went on the less sure he was he said anything that made sense. He heard the *crack, crack, cracks* of the ruler on his ass and himself yelling out things that might have been numbers. At the point he thought should be fifty, Mistress Kaho kept on striking him.

She stopped. "You mistook your count. But I did not."

Brant's face clenched tight with the burning. "I'm sorry, Mistress."

"I know you are. And thrilled too, I think."

Brant felt her hand reach under his left hip and take hold of his penis. She squeezed it playfully a couple of times and let go.

He heard the sound of a bottle clicking open and something being squeezed. A sudden coldness soothed the burning in his rear as Mistress Kaho rubbed lotion over his punished backside. Brant lay over her knees, naked, cock ramrod erect, and enjoyed every second of her attentions.

The warm reverie was broken by the sound of the front door being unlocked and opened. He tried to get up.

Mistress Kaho held him down with uncanny strength. "It's all right, sweetie. It's just Miho coming home."

How Ms Nakagawa could be so offhand at being discovered by her daughter with a naked man on her lap beggared belief.

Miho entered. Brant turned his face away from her and buried it in the couch to hide his identity.

"Ahh, is that Brant?" Miho asked.

"Of course."

"I see my mother has her claws in you." Another hand caressed his behind. "He has a beautiful ass."

"His cock is delightful too."

"Have you tasted him?"

"You know I have."

"No fair!"

"You will have your share. I'll even let you have some now, but you know what you have to do."

"Oh! You know I don't want to!"

"You have to learn," her mother said. Her tone became threatening.

Miho "Humphed".

Brant felt her hand on the back of his head, his face was turned to the right and he looked into the eyes of Ms Nakagawa's daughter.

"Don't be shy. I know what you and mummy have been up to." She looked at her mother. "Please let me have some."

"Earn it."

Miho pouted. "Just a little. Pretty, pretty please."

Brant felt himself falling further out of sanity. As Miho pleaded for a taste of him, the girl's eyes glinted gold, then glowed yellow.

"For now," Mistress Kaho said. "You can aid me in entertaining our guest. Brant, darling, what would you like to do to Miho?"

"Oh ... I ... could not ask ..." No, he could not possibly ask a mother for sexual favours from her daughter.

The ruler came cracking down hard on his ass and he yelped.

"Spank him!" Mistress Kaho ordered.

"Oh, goody!" Miho squealed.

Brant felt her hand spanking his raw buttocks. The pain shot through him and he squirmed. Mistress Kaho's left arm pressed down across his upper back and held him until it stopped.

"Brant, honey," Mistress Kaho said. "We've talked about this haven't we?"

"I'm sorry, Mistress."

"Now, I'll ask you again: What would you like to do to Miho?"

"I want to lick her and kiss her and fuck her!"

"Oh, I know you do."

"Yay!" Miho shouted. She stepped back from the couch and pulled her T-shirt over her head. Underneath she wore a bra of black lace. The T-shirt hit the floor and she soon unclipped the bra.

As she got to unbuckling her belt and jeans, her mother said,

"And just how would you like to fuck her?"

"Umm... the usual..."

The ruler came slicing through the air again. Brant yelled, "AHH!" when it struck home.

"Miho," Mistress Kaho said.

Miho got her jeans off. Her black satin panties soon followed. She took these and pushed the gusset to Brant's nose. He breathed in her moist scent as Miho's hand punished him again.

When she stopped, Mistress Kaho said, "Brant?"

Brant, wincing, said, "I want to fuck her pussy! I want to fuck her in the ass!"

Miho gasped. "No!"

"You will do as you are told!" Mistress Kaho shouted. "But for now," she continued in a quieter tone. "Lick his asshole. He enjoys that, don't you Brant?"

"Yes, Mistress."

The cushions of the couch moved as Miho got behind him. Her hands took his buttocks and held them open. Her face pressed to his behind, her cheeks pushed hard to his butt cheeks and her tongue teased his anus.

Mistress Kaho's fingers ran through his hair. "Now. What do you want to do next?"

"I want to kiss you both, taste you both, and fuck you both."

Mistress Kaho chuckled. "You are learning."

Brant was not sure what he was doing. He lay over the older woman's lap with his posterior on fire, while her daughter's face pushed between his buttocks. Amid all this, he could only tell the truth about what he wanted. Each time he did, he moved further out of the world, and maybe further out of his mind.

"Get up," Mistress Kaho said.

Miho got up and Brant followed her. Mistress Kaho stood up and faced him. Miho stood beside her.

"And?" Mistress Kaho said.

Brant moved forward, took her breasts in his hands, and squeezed. He kissed her. Mistress Kaho sucked his tongue. With her lips wrapped around it, she drew back. A trail of saliva dripped from their mouths and wet his chest.

Brant turned to Miho, took hold of the younger woman's breasts and squeezed hard as he kissed her. Mistress Kaho's mouth was like fine, aged wine, her daughter's was fresher, her lips smaller and more delicate. Both experiences were divine.

Brant turned to Mistress Kaho. "Suck me."

She knelt.

Miho watched her mother fellate him. Her breasts small but prominent, her nipples maroon dark against her pale skin. Between her legs, her pubic hair was thin but wide. Brant felt a weird combination of embarrassment and excitement at being sucked by Mistress Kaho while her daughter looked on.

"Do you like me?" Miho asked. She turned around for him to see her from behind. Her back was artwork, perfect lines of the female human form down to her small, delectable buttocks. She bent forward and he saw the secret places between her cheeks and thighs. A tiny, pale anal ring and slim labia glistening with moisture. Silver glints of clear fluid ran down the inside of her legs.

"You're beautiful."

Miho stood up, turned back to him and came closer. She sat on the floor by her mother.

Mistress Kaho released his cock and Miho took her place. Mistress Kaho moved behind him. He felt her tongue slip into his ass.

He stood there between the older and younger women as they lapped at his body in front and behind. It was a paradise of sensations he was incredibly privileged to. The thought of the possible cost of it came to him and his shoulders tensed. The night was wonderful and strange; he could not credit himself being the man to experience it. He looked down at Miho as she moved and bobbed her head forward and back along his penis. There should have been surprise and fear at the twisted black horns coming from her scalp. He felt only acceptance. Whatever happened now, he would enjoy it, he decided. It was like stepping off a cliff and hoping there might be a net below him.

Miho pulled her mouth back off him. Her eyes raised to his, they glowed bright yellow. "Will you fuck me now, Brant darling?"

Mistress Kaho withdrew her tongue from his anus. "Not you, not yet." Her mouth planted a kiss on his right buttock, then nipped him with her teeth.

Miho pouted like a little girl but said nothing.

"Lay on the couch, Brant," Mistress Kaho said, patting his behind.

Brant did as he was told. Mistress Kaho, her horns now as visible as her daughter's, straddled him, her left knee tight between his body and the back of the couch, her right foot she braced on the floor. She lowered herself down and Brant's cock slid inside her. A long 'ah...' escaped her as she penetrated herself and moved her hips. Her face contorted, and she grunted out her pleasure.

Miho watched her mother fuck him. To Brant, she said, "Lick my pussy, honey," and then got up to straddle his face in a reversed position, facing her mother. His nose rubbed her anus, his mouth opened, and he tasted the wetness of her sex. He reached up and fumbled around on Miho's body until he found her breasts. He got her nipples between his fingertips and pinched. She squealed, adding her voice to her mother's increasing expressions of ecstasy.

Mistress Kaho thrust harder. Her hands, supporting her weight on his chest, pinched his nipples hard. Brant yelped from the sudden pain; his voice muffled by Miho's wet pussy on his mouth.

Mistress Kaho yelled out words he could not understand. A primal language of guttural sounds, Brant heard screeches and grunts. The sound of it vibrated his penis and sent waves of tingles throughout his body.

Miho's voice joined her mother's. Between her thighs, Brant could make out fragments in English. A gibberish of dirty talk expressed in an alien cacophony.

Brant's penis reached a redline state, to the point of no return, but held. Underneath Miho's sex, his face grimaced and he groaned from an orgasm that did not occur. He yelled into Miho's pussy along with the two women. Mistress Kaho's thrusting increased to an inhuman level, hammering his body into the couch.

It was a miracle he did not reach orgasm. It was a wonder nothing broke beneath her sexual power.

Mistress Kaho stopped; her body shuddered. She screamed, "*Oh! Oh! Coming!*"

She came all over him. Miho rose and between her legs, he saw Mistress Kaho lift herself and hot yellow fluid fountained from her sex onto his penis and stomach. Miho masturbated her pussy inches from his face and unleashed another stream of hot feminine ejaculate over him.

Mistress Kaho, panting, climbed off him. Miho followed. Brant wiped his face and sat up, relieved his body could still move.

"My turn!" Miho said.

"No," her mother said.

"What! That's not fair!"

"Then you know what you have to do."

"But!"

"I've had enough of your procrastinating!" Mistress Kaho bellowed. "Over the back of the couch now!"

"No, mama, please!"

"Now!"

Miho lowered her eyes, glanced around the floor and hugged herself. Hesitantly she went to the couch. She glanced at Brant once as she got onto her knees and leaned over the back of it, presenting her ass to her mother.

"Brant, go around to the other side and hold her hands."

Brant obeyed. Not sure if he should stay or leave, he took Miho's wrists in his hands and pulled them out straight. He had a pang of guilt over holding the girl down so she could be punished, but his desire was greater. He wanted to see what would happen next; he wanted to be a part of it.

"No, mama, please."

Mistress Kaho went to the cabinet and returned with a length of soft black rope. She bound her daughter's ankles and knees together.

"Brant, my daughter has put this off for far too long. She needs to have her anal virginity taken, and you are just the person to do it. But for the moment, she needs a good spanking. Hold her tight, she likes to kick."

Mistress Kaho picked up the long wooden ruler from where it lay on the floor.

"No, mama. Not too many, please! I'll do it! I'll let him fuck my asshole!"

Mistress Kaho took up a striking position behind her daughter. "Yes, you will. But I think you need this all the same. Twenty-five from me, and twenty-five from Brant, for making him wait."

"Oh mama, please, no!"

Mistress Kaho swung the ruler. For a second, beside her horns, bat-like wings appeared on her back. And on Miho's back, the same leathery wings raised to the air.

Miho squealed at the pain and tried to twist away. Brant held her wrists.

"Count!" Mistress Kaho screamed at her.

"One, mama!"

The punishment continued, crack after crack after crack, Miho's ass wobbled from the beating, turned pink and then red. She counted the strikes near incoherently. By the time she got to twenty-five, she was crying.

"There." Mistress Kaho dropped the ruler and came around the couch to take her daughter's wrists from Brant. "Now, finish the punishment."

"Please, Brant, no!" Miho cried. "I'll let you fuck my little asshole, I will. You can slide it up me all you want. I don't care if it hurts!"

"Yes, you will," Mistress Kaho said grimly.

Brant walked to the wooden ruler. His cock as hard as the wood of the implement he bent to pick up. He took aim Miho's reddened behind.

He swung.

"Twenty-six!" Miho squealed.

Brant told himself he would be gentle. He moved the strokes lower down to the back of her thighs, an area not yet burning red.

He swung and swung. *Crack! Crack! Crack!*

"Fifty!" Miho just barely said when the last strike hit her. She sobbed.

Mistress Kaho stroked her hair. "There now, all finished my dear. Don't you feel so much better?"

"Yes, mama," Miho said between sobs. "Will Brant fuck me now?"

"Why don't you ask him?"

"Brant, please fuck me," Miho begged through her tears. "Please fuck my asshole."

"Fuck her pussy first," Mistress Kaho said. "Make her come before you sodomise her. I will allow you to bugger me first, to show her there is nothing to be afraid of." She came around to Brant's side of the couch and unbound her daughter's legs. Once the ropes came off, Miho moved her knees apart and lowered herself a little.

Going further into the dream, Brant knelt on the couch behind her. The fluids from her sex ran down the inside of her thighs in rivulets. He took hold of her hips, put his cock to her pussy, and pushed in.

Miho squealed. "Oh, at last! Brant, honey, fuck me! Fuck me silly!"

He moved with all the desire the spanking fired in him; he released it in his movements and fucked her hard and fast and in a way he never thought he could.

Miho screamed, this time from aroused pleasure. The slim girl wriggled and twisted. She slammed her hips back into him with the same force he slammed into her and when she came, she arched her back and howled at the ceiling.

He stopped moving, still inside her, and leaned forward. His sweat rubbed off his chest onto her back.

"Well done, my sweets," Mistress Kaho said. She went to the cabinet and came back with a large tube of lubricant. She handed the lubricant to Brant and got onto her knees beside her daughter, and leaned over the back of the couch in the same way.

Brant pulled out of Miho. He shifted his position to behind Mistress Kaho's larger ass and opened the tube. He squirted some onto his penis and coated it, then closed the tube and put it beside them.

"Put it in my ass, Brant, sweetie."

He slid the head of his cock up and down the crevice between Mistress Kaho's buttocks a few times, rubbing it over her puckered ring.

Miho shifted her position and moved to watch up close.

Brant slid the tip of his cock to Mistress Kaho's anus and pushed.

Mistress Kaho let out a long, deep, "Ohhhh..." as his cock made its way up her tight passage.

"Oh mama, how does it feel?"

"Ahh... delightful," Mistress Kaho said as if she were enjoying a long massage, rather than a slow buggering.

Brant pushed up into her as far as he could, his thighs pushed against hers, and then he withdrew. When his glans began to pull back past her sphincter, he drove into her again with more speed. He held her hips and began to thrust.

Mistress Kaho threw back her head and yelled with each shove of his cock. Her ponytail whipped about her shoulders, her legs went wide on the couch and flailed as he skewered her again and again.

"Frig! Me!" she shouted between thrusts.

"Yes, mama!" Miho reached between her mother's legs and dutifully masturbated her.

Brant could not tell how long he pumped his body into her. At the edge of his awareness, beneath Mistress Kaho's shouts and grunts, was the slow ticking of the old clock. The sound faded as his mind slipped into a place outside of time. Their bodies, joined by his cock pistoning in and out of her anal passage, became a chimera. His senses knew only the screaming of his pleasure combined with hers. Miho's arm moved with the speed of a hummingbird's wings rubbing her mother's clitoris, driving her to cosmic levels of pleasure.

"*Coming!*" Mistress Kaho screamed to the ceiling. She collapsed over the back of the couch, breathing hard. Her body spasmed.

Brant could not believe he had not come with her, or long before. He pulled out and tried to catch his breath. He did not have long.

Miho grabbed the lotion off the couch and squeezed more of it onto his cock. She dropped the tube without replacing the cap and got back onto her knees over the back of the couch next to her mother. "Do me now, Brant! Fuck my little hole!"

Brant moved behind her. He slid the head up and down and found her anus.

Miho squealed. The passage was tighter than her mother's, he worked his way into her more carefully. Each little push took him further into Miho's back passage and elicited more squeals from her.

"You are splitting me in two!"

Brant stopped and waited.

"Don't stop! Push your cock all the way into me!"

Brant pushed until his thighs hit the back of hers. Miho's body shivered from her toes to her shoulders.

Mistress Kaho recovered herself and sat back on the couch to watch them. She reached beneath her daughter's legs and found her clitoris.

Brant took hold of Miho's slim hips and fucked her.

Miho shouted and kicked her feet. She slammed her fists into the back of the couch and yelled. *"Fucking fuck me in the fucking —ahh!—asshole! Fucking dirty! Fuck this girl's little bumhole! Dirty fucking boy!"* From that her screeches came in the incomprehensible animal language.

The more she screamed at him, the more Brant wanted to fuck her. He slammed harder and harder into her backside, faster and faster. He violated her with increasing aggressiveness, made her small body flail about, forcing his pleasure into her, forcing it from her. Miho's screamed abuse goaded him to ravish her to extremes. Mistress Kaho frigged her daughter's clitoris and grinned at them both with glowing eyes.

Whatever magic he drew from the succubi left him and he could not take anymore. The nerves in his cock screamed along with Miho. The heart of their bestial fucking burst and the pressure, the crisis, blasted out, shuddering his body.

"Don't come inside her!" Mistress Kaho shouted.

Brant barely registered her words but pulled out of her daughter and got to his feet off the couch micro-seconds before his cock spat its load. Mistress Kaho grabbed the jerking thing between his legs and put her face to it with her mouth open. Miho spun around in a blur of movement and dropped to the floor next to her mother. Both women took the blasts of semen on their faces. Not one gobbet missed them. They sucked his come into their mouths with loud slurping noises. What semen that did go astray and dropped to their breasts they cleaned off each other with long slow laps of their tongues.

Brant watched, dazed, as they kissed each other, swirling the sticky white fluid with their tongues in each other's mouths before they both swallowed.

"Oh my god."

The two women grinned at him, their eyes glowing yellow beneath the unnatural headdresses of the twisted black horns. The bat wings became visible and flapped. They screeched and chattered erratically in their demonic tongue between lapping up stray drops of his semen off each other.

The vision faded. Everything faded as he passed out.

Brant woke up in a bed. He saw moonlight and the shadow of giant bat wings above him. He tensed and started to back himself away.

"Relax, sweetie," Mistress Kaho said. "Don't be afraid." She moved up the bed and straddled him. Within the shadow of her face, the twin yellow embers of her eyes burned until she came into the moonlight and the yellow glow became a glint of gold.

"What are you?" His heart thudded fast. He still wanted to move away but her weight on his hips pinned him.

She reached down and took his hands and placed them on her breasts. With minds of their own, they kneaded the soft flesh automatically. His fingers found her nipples and squeezed.

"Relax," she whispered. "No harm will come to you. None that you don't want. You already know what we are."

Brant looked at her and knew she spoke the truth. The horns and wings were proof enough. "Does this night ever end?"

"That depends on you. Do you want it to end?"

"No. Not yet."

"Good. There is still yet more for us to do. Miho has gone out for me, to get a surprise for you. In the meantime, come and bathe with me."

The tub was already filled with steaming water when they entered the bathroom. In addition to horns and wings, Mistress Kaho now also sported a long black pointed tail that grew from her body at the top of her buttocks. All these succubi appendages vanished, however, just as she closed the bathroom door.

She took a pink plastic basin and scooped some of the hot water out and poured it down Brant's body. She did this a few more times and then took a sponge and squeezed body soap onto it from a bottle on a shelf. Mistress Kaho washed him with slow, tender movements.

Later, Brant rested in the warm water of Mistress Kaho's bathtub. She sat between his legs, leaning back into him. Brant cupped her breasts. He began to fall asleep.

"The night is not yet over, sweetie." She got up. "Come on, I will dry you."

Brant got out of the bathtub and stood still for her. She moved around his body, drying every part of him.

When she finished, she handed him a bathrobe. "Miho is back with your present. Go and see her in the living room. I will join you shortly."

Brant entered the living room wearing the bathrobe, but when he saw what was waiting for him there, he felt naked.

Miho sat on the arm of the couch, one leg stretched across the back. She wore tight black leather shorts that scarcely covered her underwear. Or would not have covered her underwear, Brant could not be sure she wore any. Black fishnet pantyhose covered her legs. Over her breasts, she wore a leather bra. Her midriff was bare.

Stephanie sat on the couch in front of her in a Batgirl T-shirt and blue jeans. When Brant entered, she looked up at him with wide eyes. "What are you doing here?"

"He is my special guest," Mistress Kaho said from behind him. She entered the room wearing a black see-through bodystocking embroidered in floral patterns around her breasts. Simple straps over her bare shoulders held the piece up. The garment was crotchless, and she wore no underwear.

In her hand, Mistress Kaho held a leather flogger whip.

Stephanie looked at her and said nothing.

"Stephanie, here," Mistress Kaho said in her school ma'am voice. "Is indebted to me, aren't you dear?"

Stephanie nodded.

"To the tune of some two thousand dollars, isn't that right? She has a rather unfortunate habit, Brant. Stephanie likes to make bets."

"Yes, Mistress Kaho." Stephanie looked down at the floor.

Brant felt himself slipping further into the bizarre sexual world of the succubus. Stephanie addressed Ms Nakagawa as 'Mistress Kaho' and did not react to the older woman's costume at all.

"I am going to make an offer to you, Stephanie," Mistress Kaho said. "A plan that will allow you to work off your debt to me, without having to return any of the money you owe. Does that interest you?"

"I guess."

"Very well. It is this: You will come here when I summon you and do anything and everything that I instruct you to. Each time you will work off ten per cent of the loan."

"Okay," Stephanie said.

"Furthermore. Once you have agreed, and we have begun, you will refuse none of my directions. If you do, I will add more to the amount that you have to work off, and I will punish you." As she said the last part, she ran the strands of the flogger whip through her fingers, making her meaning clear.

Stephanie's eyes went wide. "But—"

Mistress Kaho cut her off. "Choose."

Stephanie looked at the floor and gave a slight nod.

"Say it!"

"I agree."

"Good. You will begin now by removing your clothes."

Stephanie glanced at Brant. "I can't!"

"Your first refusal. That is already ten strokes with my flogger."

Stephanie's jaw dropped, but she did not move off the couch or try to leave.

"We're waiting." Mistress Kaho's eyes glowed, the horns and bat wings became visible.

Brant watched Stephanie closely. Could she see, as he could, what kind of creature Mistress Kaho was?

Stephanie looked at the floor and nodded again. She stood up, glanced at Brant, and pulled her T-Shirt over her head. Her breasts in their white bra lifted, dropped and bounced a little as she lowered her arms. The T-Shirt dropped to the floor and Stephanie unbuckled the belt of her jeans, unbuttoned them and lowered the zipper. She pushed the jeans down her legs and lifted her feet out of them.

When next she stood straight, Brant's penis stirred and awoke. He had wanted to see Stephanie like this for a long time. He knew he should try to help her, to offer to pay her debt and take her home. But his desire got the better of him once more. He quashed the guilt and let his lust have its way.

Without raising her eyes from the floor, Stephanie unhooked her bra and her breasts popped free. Her dark nipples stood tall.

Stephanie paused her undressing. She glanced in Brant's direction without meeting his eyes.

"You aren't finished," Mistress Kaho said. "Ten more strokes."

"Oh!" Stephanie pushed her panties down and stepped out of them.

She stood straight and everyone took the time to appreciate her naked form. Deep, black hair covered her mons.

Miho got off her perch on the couch and moved around to the

front. "She has a delightful ass."

"Turn around and bend over," Mistress Kaho said.

Stephanie turned, bent and touched her toes. Her labia glistened in the light.

"Is it everything you imagined?" Mistress Kaho asked him.

"Better." His cock poked out of the bathrobe.

Stephanie began to straighten.

"Did I tell you could stand?" Mistress Kaho said.

Stephanie resumed her toe-touching position.

Mistress Kaho stepped toward her. She swished the flogger around in the air a couple of times, then dangled the tips of the leather strands over Stephanie's ass, tickling her with them.

"Now, I think it is time to take those twenty strokes," Mistress Kaho said. "Let's make it thirty, shall we? For standing up before you were told."

"No! Please!"

"I can make it forty if you like."

Stephanie remained silent.

"Ten from me. Ten from my daughter, and ten from Brant here. Oh, and when we are done with that, Brant would very much like to fuck you."

Stephanie gasped and almost stood straight again.

"*Everything* you are instructed by me to do, you will *do*," Mistress Kaho reminded her. She held the flogger in her left hand and ran the middle finger of her right up and down between Stephanie's labia. She slipped the finger into Stephanie's pussy up to the knuckle.

Stephanie let out a little yelp but held her position.

"And you are quite ready for him too," Mistress Kaho murmured. "Very well, we shall begin. Stand up, kneel on the couch and lean over the back."

Stephanie obeyed, she glanced back at Brant for a moment, before assuming the position as instructed.

"Hold her hands, Brant, dear," Mistress Kaho said. "Oh, and you can take the robe off."

Brant dropped the robe off his shoulders and with it any lingering doubts. He moved to the back of the couch and took hold of Stephanie's wrists. She watched Brant's cock swing with his movements, just centimetres from her face.

Miho undressed. Her leather bra dropped; her leather shorts followed. She did have underwear, a red G-String under her fishnet pantyhose. She peeled the pantyhose off just as Mistress Kaho swung.

The air cracked with the flogger's impact on Stephanie's posterior. Stephanie squealed and tried to twist away. Brant held her.

"Count them, you little bitch, or maybe I will just keep going and going!"

"One!"

Mistress Kaho resumed the punishment. Her arm moved with professional efficiency, the cracks came again and again. Poor Stephanie squealed out the numbers.

"Ten!"

Mistress Kaho handed the whip to Miho. Mistress Kaho stepped back and masturbated.

Miho swung as fast and efficiently as her mother.

"Eleven!" Stephanie wailed. "Twelve-thirteen-fourteen-fifteen-sixte-seven-! AHH! AHH! AHH!"

Stephanie's legs and buttocks trembled by the time she finished the second ten.

"I don't think we can count those last three, can we dear?" Mistress Kaho said. "Count properly."

Miho swung the flogger into Stephanie's ass three more times. Stephanie shouted the numbers.

Mistress Kaho came to stand by Brant. She took Stephanie's wrists. "Your turn, Brant, sweetie."

He walked around to the front of the couch. Stephanie's pearly white backside was glowing pink now. Miho handed him the whip, then sat on the couch next to Stephanie with her legs up and fingered herself.

Brant ran his hands over the round globes of Stephanie's punished behind, feeling the warmth come off it.

"He's going to fuck you right after he finishes," Mistress Kaho said. "He's going to slide his cock right up into you where you are now. I think he is going to need it soon, he's so very hard. He already fucked me, and Miho here. He fucked us and then he buggered us. Perhaps he should poke it up your tight back passage, Stephanie dear."

"No, I don't do that!"

"You will do what I tell you. Miho didn't want to be sodomised either. But she was."

"That's right," Miho said. "He poked his perfect cock right up my asshole. I bounced around like a puppet on a stick."

"No, please!"

"All right, dear," Mistress Kaho said. "Not tonight." Then she added in a voice like cold steel, "But you will. We have many more nights ahead of us."

Brant stood back and raised his arm. He swung.

"AHH! Twenty-one!" Stephanie screamed. "Twenty-two! Twenty-three! Twenty-four!"

Brant went slower than Mistress Kaho or Miho. He did not have the practised skill of the succubi and, truth be told, he wanted to savour it.

"Thirty!"

"Now beg him," Mistress Kaho said. "Beg him to fuck you."

"Please fuck me, Brant!"

Brant dropped the whip, kneeled on the couch, and slid into Stephanie's cunt.

"OH!"

He took her hips and thrust hard and fast. Mistress Kaho released Stephanie's hands and widened her stance to masturbate along with her daughter.

Brant fucked on and on, watching the two succubi pleasure themselves. Their magic seeped back into him, he thrust with impossible speed.

"Tell her, Brant," Mistress Kaho said. "Tell her what you feel."

"I've wanted to fuck you for so long, Stephanie," he grunted.

"How does her cunt feel?"

"Her cunt is so tight, so wet."

Stephanie's voice came in low, "Hm! Hm! Hm!" sounds with each thrust into her.

"Open your mouth, Stephanie dear," Mistress Kaho said. "Let us hear your pleasure."

"No, I'm not feeling... Ah!"

"But you are, I can see it. I saw your face when he penetrated you. I can see your face now."

Brant stopped, drew back and slammed in hard.

"Ah... shit!" Stephanie grunted.

"You felt that, didn't you dear? Pound her again, Brant."

Brant drew back and slammed hard. The couch jerked across the floorboards.

"AH!"

"Her mouth is open now, Brant darling. You liked that didn't you, Stephanie?'

Brant began pounding as hard as he could.

"OH! OH! OH! OH!"

Mistress Kaho took her hand from her pussy and touched Stephanie's face. She brought it up and showed him the spit on her fingers. "She's enjoying it so much, she's drooling. You're going to come, aren't you, Stephanie dear?"

Stephanie's voice, her yells, came at a higher pitch. "*AH! AH! AH!*"

"I'm going to come too," Miho said. "Let me show you." Miho stood on the couch by Stephanie. She raised her right leg to the backrest and masturbated furiously. "Oh fuck!" She ejaculated. A golden stream splashed onto Stephanie's hair and ran down her back.

"What a good idea." Mistress Kaho raised her right leg to the couch's backrest. With her pussy to Stephanie's face she said, "Keep her mouth open, Brant."

Another stream of female come fountained from Mistress Kaho. The fluid hit Stephanie's face making her screams into splutters. Both the succubi ejaculated again, simultaneously drenching her.

"Shit! I'm going to come!" Stephanie screamed.

So was Brant, and somehow, the two succubi knew it.

"Come on her face!" Mistress Kaho ordered.

Brant pulled out, Stephanie spun around and slid off the couch to her knees on the floor and waited with her eyes closed.

Brant's orgasm wracked through him. His body shuddered as he ejaculated spurt after spurt onto Stephanie. It hit her face, went up her nose, into her hair. More hit her chin, her neck and ran down her breasts.

Mistress Kaho and Miho came and slurped it off her like wild dogs licking up the blood of slain prey. Their wings flapped triumphantly; their tails flicked in the air like whips.

Brant dropped to his knees. The last thing he saw was the look of absolute delight on Stephanie's face as the sex monsters licked his come off her.

He awoke with his cheek resting on something warm. He opened his eyes and saw he was lying on the couch with his head resting on Stephanie's ass. Their clothes were scattered around the living room floor. Watching Stephanie sleep, an enormous pang of guilt shot through him. He had whipped her and then fucked her without hesitation. The red marks across her buttocks belonged in part to him. The extreme arousal now faded, the shame and guilt could no longer be suppressed. The succubi had summoned up a lust in him that made him into a beast.

He got up and went to the window. Night had passed, but so had the day. The sky glowed orange from the sunset. An entire day of work gone. He returned to the couch and shook Stephanie's shoulder.

She stirred and got up. Rubbing her eyes, she said, "What time is it?"

"Sunset, I think. Listen, I'm ... really sorry about ..."

"Sunset? Shit, we have to get out of here!" Stephanie began snatching up her clothes. "Hurry up! Get dressed before they come back."

Brant joined her in pulling his clothes back on. "I don't know what happened last night," he said as he buckled his pants on. "Things got really out of control."

"They are succubi, Brant. If they come back, things will get really out of control again. Let's go."

They went to the front door. Brant took the handle to turn it. It did not move.

At all.

It did not rattle or rotate; the doorknob was fixed solid. He tried shaking the door. Nothing moved. For the first time since being drawn into the world of the succubi, Brant felt genuine fear.

Stephanie tried the door. "We're trapped."

Brant went back to the living room to try the windows. The latches on all of them were fixed as solidly as the doorknob.

"We can't leave because you don't want to," Stephanie said.

"Of course I want to!"

"No, Brant. You have to want to leave."

Stephanie's voice sounded odd. He turned and found her undressing.

"What the hell are you doing?"

She stood up from pushing her jeans down. Naked once more, she raised her face. Two yellow eyes looked back at him. Above them, twisted horns adorned her head. Wings unfurled from her back and flapped twice. The wind they made ruffled Brant's hair.

"You can't be," he whispered.

Stephanie grinned. "You fucked me like a beast, Brant darling. I want more."

Mistress Kaho entered the room in her full succubus form. In the increasing dark, the glowing yellow eyes burned bright. "My daughter is quite right, Brant. You cannot leave here unless you truly want to. And you don't, do you?"

Hands reached around him from behind. One pinched his left nipple through his shirt, the other cupped his groin and squeezed.

"The night of the succubus is long," Miho whispered in his ear.

"You said no harm would come to me." Brant's heart thudded. He had summoned demons into his life, to grant his wishes. Now he knew the price.

"Nothing you don't want," Mistress Kaho said. "And you have wanted all of it. And more still."

Stephanie and Mistress Kaho came closer. Miho unbuckled his trousers; they dropped to the floor. She took hold of Brant's cock. His erection, betraying him, returned with a vengeance.

"Men like you are a speciality of ours," Mistress Kaho said. "I think we are going to be together for a long time."

The succubi closed in around him.

CPSIA information can be obtained
at www.ICGtesting.com
Printed in the USA
BVHW051824010722
641150BV00011B/124

9 781709 491351